Origin Story

by Nathan Alan Davis

No one shall make any changes in this title(s) for the purpose of production. No part of this book may be reproduced, stored in a retrieval system, scanned, uploaded, or transmitted in any form, by any means, now known or yet to be invented, including mechanical, electronic, digital, photocopying, recording, videotaping, or otherwise, without the prior written permission of the publisher. No one shall share this title(s), or any part of this title(s), through any social media or file hosting websites.

For all inquiries regarding motion picture, television, online/digital and other media rights, please contact Concord Theatricals Corp.

MUSIC AND THIRD-PARTY MATERIALS USE NOTE

Licensees are solely responsible for obtaining formal written permission from copyright owners to use copyrighted music and/or other copyrighted third-party materials (e.g. artworks, logos) in the performance of this play and are strongly cautioned to do so. If no such permission is obtained by the licensee, then the licensee must use only original music and materials that the licensee owns and controls. Licensees are solely responsible and liable for clearances of all third-party copyrighted materials, including without limitation music, and shall indemnify the copyright owners of the play(s) and their licensing agent, Concord Theatricals Corp., against any costs, expenses, losses and liabilities arising from the use of such copyrighted third-party materials by licensees. For music, please contact the appropriate music licensing authority in your territory for the rights to any incidental music.

IMPORTANT BILLING AND CREDIT REQUIREMENTS

If you have obtained performance rights to this title, please refer to your licensing agreement for important billing and credit requirements.

ORIGIN STORY received its world premiere at Cincinnati Playhouse in the Park, (Blake Robison, Producing Artistic Director; Abby Marcus, Managing Director) on May 20, 2023. The production was directed by Joanie Schultz, with set design by Chelsea M. Warren, costume design by Izumi Inaba, lighting design by Heather Gilbert, and sound design & original music by T. Carlis Roberts. The stage manager was Andrea L. Shell. The cast was as follows:

MARGARET . . . . Amira Danan

VAL. . . . . Betsy Hogg

ANITA . . . . Shonita Joshi

BOBBY. . . . . .Michael Lepore

DEX. . . . . Josh Odor

ROXANNE. . . . . Dwandra Nickole Lampkin

GARY . . . . Bill Timoney

ORIGIN STORY received a developmental workshop at DETOUR: A Festival of New Work at WaterTower Theatre in Addison, Texas, in 2018.

A workshop production of *ORIGIN STORY* was produced by the Department of Theatre Arts & Dance at Sonoma State University, directed by Delicia Turner Sonnenberg.

CHARACTERS

MARGARET – (W, 30s, ethnically ambiguous) Works at The Services Corporation during the day. Also works the graveyard shift at The Burg.

VAL – (W, 30s, white) Works at The Services Corporation with Margaret.

ANITA – (W, 20s, Tamil) Works at The Services Corporation in the HR department.

BOBBY – (M, 20s, white) Works the graveyard shift at The Burg with Margaret.

DEX – (M, 42) Val's lover on Mondays.

ROXANNE – (W, 40s–50s, black) A regular drive-thru customer at The Burg.

GARY – (M, 50s–60s, white) A Xerox repairman.

SETTING

An American city.

TIME

The present.

AUTHOR'S NOTE

The people in this play might be described as weird, and much of what they do is very silly. That said, they don't think of themselves this way. They, generally, take themselves seriously. Resist the temptation to wink and nod (literally or metaphorically) at the comedy.

An ellipsis on its own line

...

represents a pause, a beat, or perhaps a physical action.

A slash / marks the beginning of an overlap.

SPECIAL THANKS

Joanie Shultz, for so deeply believing in this play and embracing all its silliness.

Delicia Turner-Sonnenberg, for your wisdom and advocacy.

Michael Castalez, for your *Star Wars Episode VII* analysis that became a provocation for this piece.

One

Monday morning, The Services Corporation.

> (**MARGARET** *and* **VAL** *stand around a water cooler. They hold tiny paper cups, which they sip from occasionally.*)
>
> (*But mostly they stare at the water cooler. It's almost as if the water cooler is a campfire. But they are not at a campground. They are in an office building where they work.*)

VAL. How was your weekend?

MARGARET. …

…

You know it's like: I would love to be able to answer that question…

VAL. Right?

MARGARET. Yeah.

…

VAL. Life: what is it?

MARGARET. It's like I can't even go to the grocery store.

VAL. …

Why can't you go to the grocery store?

MARGARET. The girl checking out my groceries?

VAL. Yeah?

MARGARET. She looks at me and she goes – she doesn't even say "hi," by the way. No "hi" no "did you find everything you needed" none of that.

She looks at me,

VAL. Yeah?

MARGARET. And she says,

"What are you?"

VAL. Ew.

MARGARET. Yeah.

VAL. Like,

MARGARET. Yeah.

VAL. Racially?

MARGARET. Yes.

VAL. Ew.

MARGARET. Yeah.

VAL. That's so –

MARGARET. I know –

VAL. Yuck.

MARGARET. Anyway.

VAL. White people: we're the worst.

MARGARET. This chick wasn't white!

VAL. No?

MARGARET. No.

VAL. ...

We do say that a lot, though. My people.

We say that shit all the time.

MARGARET. I know you do.

VAL. We think it even more than we say it.

MARGARET. Everyone thinks it.

VAL. We think it hard, though.

...

We try not to think it, but it's like...

MARGARET. ...

VAL. So.

...

What did you tell her?

MARGARET. Hm?

VAL. She said, "What are you?"

MARGARET. Uhuh.

VAL. And you said:

...

MARGARET. I don't know I said whatever I said and I took my groceries and got out of there.

VAL. ...

Margaret?

MARGARET. Yes, Val?

VAL. I feel uncomfortable about asking this question.

MARGARET. Uhuh.

VAL. 'Cause we've been working together for like, what three years?

MARGARET. Two-and-a-half.

VAL. Yeah, so you know...

I mean I consider you a friend. Right?

MARGARET. Definitely.

VAL. Yeah.

>   And like you generally
>
>   Know certain things.
>
>   About a person who is a friend.

MARGARET. …

VAL. Like I've never met your parents, for example.

MARGARET. I don't actually know my ethnicity.

VAL. …

>   What do you mean?

MARGARET. I mean I don't know.

>   I was adopted by very loving, very red-headed protestants.
>
>   I don't know who my birth parents were.

VAL. Oh.

MARGARET. …

VAL. Cool.

>   …
>
>   I mean, not "cool" but like…

MARGARET. …

VAL. Have you ever tried to find out?

>   You know there's…you can take one of those DNA tests.

MARGARET. Gross, no.

VAL. Why not?

MARGARET. Because gross. And because no.

VAL. It would be exciting!

MARGARET. Not for me.

VAL. It would be like an ultrasound when you find out the sex of the baby! I'd hold your hand and everything.

MARGARET. ...

I've always just thought of myself as human.

VAL. Oh.

Yeah definitely don't do it then.

MARGARET. Thanks, I won't.

VAL. Yeah, 'cause I did mine? Did I tell you this?

MARGARET. No.

VAL. Yeah, I did mine and I'm like,

Not 100% human.

MARGARET. I don't think that's...

VAL. I'm part Neanderthal.

As are a lot of people actually.

MARGARET. Really?

VAL. Yeah, I'm not kidding.

MARGARET. Okay.

But that's like...

VAL. ...

MARGARET. That's still human.

VAL. Is it?

MARGARET. I mean it kind of has to be. Right?

VAL. I guess.

MARGARET. ...

VAL. Do you think of me differently now?

MARGARET. No.

VAL. You totally do.

MARGARET. Of course I don't!

VAL. Okay, well, how about to you I'm Val. And you won't worry what percentage Neanderthal I am.

And to me, you're Margaret.

And we'll just agree to always look at each other that way no matter what.

MARGARET. Works for me.

VAL. Alright, cheers.

   (**MARGARET** *and* **VAL** *drink from their cups.*)

   (**MARGARET** *begins to exit.*)

Where you off to?

MARGARET. My cubicle.

VAL. What're you planning on getting done today?

MARGARET. I mean probably not a whole lot, until someone inevitably asks me to help them with the copier.

   (**ANITA** *enters and walks straight to the water cooler. She stands near* **VAL** *and* **MARGARET** *and drinks. She's wearing headphones.*)

VAL. Yeah, so hang out.

MARGARET. My chair is over there.

VAL. Bring it over here.

MARGARET. …

We can't bring our chairs over here.

VAL. Who says?

MARGARET. …

VAL. What're they gonna do?

Fire us?

ANITA. They might.

VAL. …

Oh, I'm sorry, were you part of this conversation?

ANITA. …

VAL. We don't know you.

ANITA. Hi, I'm Anita.

VAL. Are you listening to anything on those headphones?

ANITA. Uhuh.

VAL. What department are you in?

ANITA. Human Resources.

VAL. Oh. Okay.

Trying to scare us back to work?

Is that what's happening?

ANITA. …

VAL. HR bitch. I'm talking to you.

ANITA. Anita.

VAL. Anita. How long have you been working here?

ANITA. Today's my first official day.

VAL. Well let me tell you something: Margaret and I: You don't scare us.

ANITA. Good.

VAL. You're not scaring us back to our desks.

ANITA. I'm not trying to.

VAL. Don't you guys have your own wing or whatever?

ANITA. I wouldn't call it a wing.

VAL. I know all about the HR wing.

ANITA. Yeah I'd call it maybe a section.

VAL. Oh, does wing feel too –

ANITA. It feels a little fancy –

VAL. I see –

ANITA. It's just a section of the building. Like any other section –

VAL. 'Cause the last time I went to HR… you know here's something you should know:

You guys make it a real *thing*.

It's a real *process* to talk with HR about something.

ANITA. Oh. I wouldn't know.

VAL. Do you know what department I work in?

ANITA. Today's my first day.

VAL. Uhuh, well I'm in marketing – which is distinct from sales by the way, I hope they told you that – And I haven't actually had any assignments for the past eighteen months, at least, because we're apparently in a "client acquisition cycle." What the hell is that?

And if I'm in marketing, and we need new clients, why am I not helping? Shouldn't that be my job?

I mean, I'm getting paid to sit around and do nothing.

And, Anita, if you or your bosses have a problem with that: Great.

I'd love to actually contribute something. And not feel useless.

ANITA. …

Interesting.

MARGARET. Welcome, Anita.

Don't take it personally, Val just has a very dramatic way of asking for things.

VAL. …

MARGARET. I'm sure you'll make this a better place.

VAL. Doubtful.

ANITA. *(To* **MARGARET.***)* Thank you.

…

MARGARET. You're welcome.

ANITA. By any chance do you work at The Burg?

MARGARET. …

Yeah.

ANITA. Yeah I saw you –

VAL. The Burg?!

MARGARET. It's not a big deal, it's just short for burger –

VAL. I know what The Burg is – you *work* there?

MARGARET. It's just a nighttime thing.

ANITA. Yeah I saw you in the drive-thru window. I was across the street / at Wendy's.

MARGARET. Across the street at Wendy's? Yeah, Wendy's is probably the safer choice.

ANITA. I remember thinking,

What's up with that girl in the drive-thru?

MARGARET. …

ANITA. She's way too glam for fast food.

MARGARET. It's an easy job.

ANITA. …

I'm gonna go back to my wing, now.

VAL. Tell your bosses they can suck it.

ANITA. Okay, I will.

VAL. Tell Sheila and Bob that they can both SUCK IT!

ANITA. I'll make sure they get the message.

VAL. I'm gonna have sex tonight. I don't know about you, but yeah it's Monday and I have this Monday thing going with this Monday guy and he and I have some real chemistry – I mean it's quite extraordinary, probably better than anything you've ever experienced in your life.

(**ANITA** *gives* **VAL** *a thumbs up.*)

ANITA. Bye, Margaret.

MARGARET. Bye.

(**ANITA** *exits.*)

VAL. (*"That was a little intimate, wasn't it?"*) Bye?

MARGARET. ...

VAL. What was going on there?

MARGARET. ...

VAL. I can't believe you work at The Burg. That place is a hellhole.

(**MARGARET** *and* **VAL** *refill their cups.*)

MARGARET. It's easy money.

VAL. How many nights a week?

MARGARET. Monday through Friday.

VAL. Girl no wonder you've been so tired!

MARGARET. I have a lot of debt.

VAL. Everyone has a lot of debt, just go bankrupt.

MARGARET. …

VAL. I can't believe you were keeping your terrible embarrassing job a secret from me. That kind of hurts, Margaret.

MARGARET. Sorry.

VAL. You have to quit.

MARGARET. …

VAL. Margaret, you really have to.

They're going to get you.

Working here is bad enough. Don't give them your whole life.

…

When do you sleep?

MARGARET. I sleep all the time. I sleep at my desk. I get a good three hours in after I get home from The Burg.

I'm basically sleeping right now. I'm good.

VAL. Go for it, then. Live your life in between the lines, exhaust yourself for no reason and die. That's what they want.

MARGARET. That's what who / wants?

VAL. And we could beat them, you know. We could actually beat them.

But people are so obsessed with getting permission.

VAL. You know what I told Chase Bank when I missed a payment?

CHASE. THIS. BITCHES!

...

And then you just don't pay.

We don't need banks. Go bankrupt. Rupture all the banks and say goodbye to them forever. No more debt. No more mortgages. If you want a house: take one.

I'm speaking from experience here.

MARGARET. You have a house?

VAL. Not a house, yet, but land. That I claimed. And which I inhabit from time to time, yes.

MARGARET. What land?

VAL. The shore of this little pond.

MARGARET. Where?

VAL. The south side. Where main street turns into state road whatever.

MARGARET. Yeah?

VAL. You hang a left there, then a quick right. There's a line of trees and if you just park on the side of the road and walk through the trees:

There's a pond.

There are ducks in it sometimes. It's great.

MARGARET. Wow.

VAL. Yeah.

Some people have secret jobs that they don't tell people about.

And I have my pond.

MARGARET. That sounds wonderful.

VAL. It is.

The only problem is that yesterday this like, I guess, man, jumped out of the pond and screamed at me.

I haven't decided yet if I can go back.

MARGARET. …

Who screamed at you?

VAL. I'm sitting there: Deep breathing. Mind clear. Eyes in soft focus, you know. Peaceful.

And then a man. This man is there in a swimming suit. Dripping wet. Screaming.

MARGARET. So what did you do?

VAL. I got the fuck out of there.

MARGARET. He just jumped out of the pond?

VAL. Yeah. Like he was some kind of, I don't know, pond swimmer, / I guess –

MARGARET. Interesting.

I have to go to the bathroom.

(**MARGARET** *exits.*)

(*The water cooler bubbles.*)

Two

Late that night. The Burg.

(**BOBBY** *and* **MARGARET** *are working at a 24-hour fast food restaurant called "The Burg." It is late at night and the inside of the restaurant is closed. Only the drive-thru window is open.* **MARGARET** *wears a headset. She is the one that takes the orders.* **BOBBY** *is the one that preps the food. But right now they're just standing around because there are no customers.*)

BOBBY. How was your weekend?

MARGARET. I think I need to start working weekends.

BOBBY. But you love your weekends.

MARGARET. But if I can get a weekend shift here then I can get a couple nights off. It's only Monday and I'm already exhausted.

BOBBY. What do you need nights off for? Just sleep more during the day. Get those curtains. You know, those light-cancelling curtains or whatever you call them.

MARGARET. Bobby, I have a real job during the day.

BOBBY. So maybe quit?

MARGARET. Why would I quit my real job? If I'm going to quit a job I'll quit this job.

BOBBY. This is a good job.

MARGARET. No it isn't.

BOBBY. But you get to hang out with me.

MARGARET. ...

BOBBY. I'm telling you, if they ever gave me that headset, I'd never give it up. I'd wear it to my funeral. Bury me in that thing, you know what I mean? Bury me in it.

MARGARET. …

BOBBY. What do you even do at your so-called real job?

MARGARET. Mostly I fix the copy machine.

BOBBY. Oh.

MARGARET. Yeah I don't know I have a knack for it.

Usually it's just a paper jam. But what people don't realize is how many places paper can potentially be jammed in. And unless you know what you're doing when you go in there, you're just as likely to cause a new problem as you are to fix the first problem. And nobody likes to call in the service guy unless it's absolutely necessary, 'cause he bothers everybody. He's always assuming we screwed up the machine by putting in an old toner cartridge. I'm like, no dude, we know what toner cartridges to put in, you tell us every freaking time you come here, the machine is breaking down because that's what it's built to do. The machine breaks down, they get paid, you get work, we get annoyed.

So anyway, yeah, I'm plan A. And plan B. Calling Xerox for the service guy is basically plan Z. So, yeah, I'm actually plans A through Y. When it comes to copy machine problems. In fact, they even – this is funny – they've started to call it a "Margaret" now. When there's a minor malfunction. Which happens quite a lot. Multiple times a day. There's nothing else for me to do anyway. We're in a client acquisition cycle.

Whatever that means.

BOBBY. You seem like you're stressed out, Margaret.

MARGARET. Do I?

BOBBY. You do.

MARGARET. That's because I have a lot on my plate.

BOBBY. Yeah that make sense.

MARGARET. …

BOBBY. Except for the fact that you don't.

You don't seem to actually have a lot on your plate.

MARGARET. I work two jobs, Bobby.

BOBBY. Right. But you don't do anything at your so-called real job –

MARGARET. Please stop calling it my so-called real job –

BOBBY. My bad, your day job –

MARGARET. No –

BOBBY. You work there during the day, right?

MARGARET. Yeah but that would imply that I have a night job.

BOBBY. This is your night job –

MARGARET. I'm saying a night job that I care about. A night calling.

BOBBY. What, like a phone sex operator?

MARGARET. No.

BOBBY. I was thinking of getting into that actually. It would pay so much better.

MARGARET. Gross.

BOBBY. Come on, you wouldn't want a sampling of my dulcet tones in the middle of the night?

MARGARET. No, people are finally safe in their beds they're not calling you.

BOBBY. What do you mean? I'm a nice dude.

MARGARET. You are a nice dude, sorry.

BOBBY. I'd be like the nice guy sexy guy. That would be my, like – that's what I would be known for in the industry. I'm sure there's totally / a market for that.

MARGARET. *(Turns on her headset.)* Welcome to the burg would you like to try one of our signature single burgs for only ninety-nine cents tonight?

…

…

I'm sorry sir our ice cream machine is down.

…

Sorry about that, yeah. There's no ice cream.

…

No. No milkshakes either.

…

Because milkshakes are ice cream.

…

…

I can put some milk in a cup and shake it.

(The sound of a car peeling away.)

BOBBY. Good one.

MARGARET. What do people expect?

BOBBY. Miracles. They actually expect miracles.

MARGARET. Wendy's is right across the street: get a Frosty and call it a night, bro.

BOBBY. That's probably what he did.

That sounded like a hard U-turn.

MARGARET. I can't handle this tonight.

BOBBY. You sure you're not like,

Going through something?

MARGARET. ...

> (**MARGARET** *takes her headset off and gives it to* **BOBBY**.)

BOBBY. What's going on?

MARGARET. I thought you said you wanted it.

BOBBY. Okay, Margaret, I know you're the shift manager and I don't want you to think that I'm challenging your authority, but I'm not trained to work the register.

MARGARET. Can you read?

BOBBY. Usually.

MARGARET. Can you push buttons?

BOBBY. Yes.

MARGARET. Congratulations, you're trained to work the register.

BOBBY. I'm seriously not giving this headset back. I hope you realize that.

MARGARET. Good. I'll never have to talk to Roxanne again.

BOBBY. Who?

MARGARET. Roxanne.

Dumbass crazy ass Roxanne.

BOBBY. You mean the lady who drives the Ford Taurus?

MARGARET. Yes. She's so extra. I think one of these nights I might actually lose it and punch her.

BOBBY. Whoa.

...

Margaret. Uh, this is…

MARGARET. …

BOBBY. Sorry. Are you black? Sorry.

MARGARET. What does that have to do with anything?

BOBBY. I'm just not sure I'm comfortable with you saying you want to punch her in the face.

MARGARET. Unless I'm black.

BOBBY. …

Yeah, basically.

I mean I don't care what race you are or whatever / I just –

MARGARET. Clearly you do care.

BOBBY. I just think it's borderline racist, the way you're talking about Roxanne; I'm not sure what makes her different from so many of our other eccentric customers except the fact that she happens to be African American.

MARGARET. She gets under my skin.

BOBBY. What about the lady who drives the Honda Accord?

MARGARET. The green Accord with the cracked windshield?

BOBBY. Yeah.

MARGARET. Okay, she's extra – but she's not Roxanne extra.

BOBBY. But why does Roxanne get under your skin if the Accord Lady doesn't?

MARGARET. First off, I don't know the Accord Lady's name.

BOBBY. Okay.

MARGARET. Because the Accord Lady doesn't introduce herself to people at drive-thru windows like Roxanne does.

BOBBY. Okay, but what about the motorcycle guy?

MARGARET. What about the motorcycle guy?!

BOBBY. He like, revs his engine in your ears.

MARGARET. He did that once. I told him not to do it again and he hasn't.

BOBBY. ...

MARGARET. Roxanne just gets to me, okay?

BOBBY. And I'm telling you maybe there's a reason for that.

MARGARET. Okay, white man, please explain my reasoning to me.

BOBBY. Wait.

So you are black? Sorry.

MARGARET. ...

BOBBY. I just.

MARGARET. ...

BOBBY. Like I don't know where I stand 'cause I don't know what...

MARGARET. ...

BOBBY. I do feel strongly that Roxanne is, uh,

That if she were white. And doing the same thing. You might be annoyed.

But I don't think you'd be so...violently upset.

MARGARET. Unless I'm black.

BOBBY. ...

Yes.

MARGARET. Because if I was black, being violently upset would just be my M.O.?

I don't...?

BOBBY. No, like. No.

Nevermind. The more I think about it the less sense it makes.

MARGARET. ...

Well maybe I'll tell you.

BOBBY. ...

MARGARET. Maybe I'll tell you what I am.

BOBBY. ...

MARGARET. If you tell me something first.

BOBBY. Okay.

MARGARET. ...

I have a feeling about you.

I get these gut feelings about things sometimes.

BOBBY. ...

Okay.

MARGARET. Do you ever do any random pond swimming?

BOBBY. Random pond swimming?

MARGARET. Yes.

BOBBY. As in...

MARGARET. As in Random. Pond. Swimming.

BOBBY. Like...pick a pond and go swim in it?

MARGARET. Yes.

BOBBY. Sure, all the time.

MARGARET. Did you do any of that last weekend?

BOBBY. Probably, I do it like every day.

MARGARET. ...

BOBBY. Doesn't everybody do that?

> (**MARGARET** *takes a picture of* **BOBBY** *with her phone.*)

MARGARET. I need to take your picture.

BOBBY. Why?

MARGARET. To send to my work friend Val to see if you're the one who scared the shit out of her over the weekend.

BOBBY. I don't scare people.

MARGARET. I had this feeling. Right when she said it, I thought: Holy shit: Bobby.

BOBBY. I don't think that's really fair.

MARGARET. I got such a strong feeling it triggered my bladder.

BOBBY. Um, okay...

MARGARET. Follow up question: When you jump out of a pond, do you scream at people?

BOBBY. Not at people.

MARGARET. But you scream.

BOBBY. Well I don't know that I'd call it a scream.

MARGARET. What would you call it?

BOBBY. I don't really call it anything.

MARGARET. But what is it?

BOBBY. It's, you know.

I sort of.

> (**BOBBY** *starts making a timid chest pounding motion.*)

MARGARET. *(Mimicking the motion.)* What is this?

BOBBY. It's,

You know I sort of give it a pound. A little chest pound.

MARGARET. And is there any vocal noise which might accompany the chest pounding?

BOBBY. Yeah, kind of a,

You know, a little, like what a barbarian would do. Kind of.

MARGARET. So you yell as loud as you can and pound your chest.

BOBBY. I guess if that's how it looks. Sure.

MARGARET. It was totally you, I'm sending this to Val.

*(**MARGARET** sends the picture.)*

BOBBY. Did I do something wrong?

MARGARET. To be determined, I guess.

BOBBY. I mean I kind of blackout sometimes when I'm screaming.

I get into this...

Not like, I'm not a werewolf or anything.

But I guess,

It's sort of embarrassing but it's kind of like a masculinity thing for me?

Like I don't find a lot of opportunities to exercise my sort of, man qualities?

BOBBY. This is weird to talk about. But yeah, I think I sometimes overdo it.

I've never hurt anybody or anything like that.

But. Like one time I stared down a duck. Like, I felt like I had to win, you know? Like, he was challenging me. I mean I know, logically, he probably wasn't. But still I couldn't make myself move until he retreated. And, I mean, he *was* looking at me. So like.

MARGARET. Good to know.

BOBBY. Yeah.

...

...

So.

MARGARET. What?

BOBBY. Nevermind.

MARGARET. Oh, yeah I was gonna tell you where I'm from.

BOBBY. I thought you were from here.

MARGARET. But like where my people are from.

BOBBY. Right.

Yeah that would be cool to know if you want to share it.

MARGARET. ...

I'm Taurisian.

BOBBY. ...

(Pretending to know what that means.)

Oh. Nice.

MARGARET. Meaning from Taurisia.

BOBBY. Right, right.

MARGARET. You've heard of it?

BOBBY. Yeah.

MARGARET. Cool. Most people haven't heard of it.

BOBBY. It's sort of, I'm not the best with geography –

MARGARET. It's okay, all Americans suck at geography.

BOBBY. Yeah, but Taurisia…it's

…

Is it near Tunisia? In that general / area?

MARGARET. Yeah.

BOBBY. Yeah that's what I thought.

Get over there to visit much?

MARGARET. Nope.

BOBBY. No family reunions or anything?

MARGARET. Not yet.

BOBBY. Cool.

I mean, honestly I don't care.

I mean I do. Like I'm glad to know where you're from. Or where your… Like where you hail from. It's cool to know.

But it's also like,

You're Margaret.

MARGARET. Thanks.

(Someone has pulled into the drive-thru lane.)

BOBBY. Oh, God, someone's here, what do I do?

MARGARET. Push the button and talk.

BOBBY. *(Into the headset.)* Hi. Good evening. Welcome to The Burg.

Would you like to try one of our single burgs for only ninety-nine cents? Tonight?

…

Sorry?

…

Bobby.

…

Bobby?

…

Yes.

…

Margaret is here, yeah. But I'll be taking your order today. Tonight.

…

Oh, okay, hi Roxanne. Nice to meet you, too.

…

Sure. Sure.

So,

Can I go ahead and take your order?

…

Two double burgs. Okay.

> (**BOBBY** *begins punching the order into the register. He's a little slow.*)

Okay, great just hold on a minute there Roxanne I'm a little –

…

No I'm okay, just first time at the register that's all.

…

Yeah. Yes. Yes that's right.

…

Margaret is training me.

…

Yeah, she is great. She's taking it easy on me. So that was two double burgs, no lettuce, extra – shit.

Sorry. Sorry, no it's not your fault I just made a mistake.

> (**MARGARET** *grabs the headset from* **BOBBY** *and puts it on.*)

MARGARET. I can't listen to this anymore. / Hi Roxanne can you go ahead and repeat your order?

BOBBY. Hey, I got this –

MARGARET. …

Bobby has been demoted back to sandwich prep, can you go ahead and repeat your order from the beginning, please?

> (**MARGARET** *punches in the order.*)

I have two double burgs, hold the lettuce, extra ketchup, light on the mayo, a large cheese fry and a large Sierra Mist. Does that complete your order?

…

$13.56 at the window.

> (**BOBBY** *makes the double burgs.* **MARGARET** *prepares the cheese fries and the Sierra Mist.*)

> (**ROXANNE** *appears at the window.*)

ROXANNE. Good evening, Margaret!!

MARGARET. Be right there!

ROXANNE. Bobby! Hey Bobby is that your name?!

BOBBY. Yeah! Just back here making your double burgs!

ROXANNE. Bobby you're doing a great job!

BOBBY. Thank you!

ROXANNE. Bobby?!

BOBBY. Yes, ma'am?!

ROXANNE. Do you have pickle relish back there?!

BOBBY. I don't believe so, no!

ROXANNE. Are you sure?!

*(**MARGARET** approaches the window.)*

MARGARET. Here's your Sierra Mist.

ROXANNE. Thank you, Margaret.

MARGARET. My pleasure.

ROXANNE. Margaret, I thought y'all had pickle relish.

MARGARET. We have packets, I'll put some in the bag for you.

ROXANNE. Bobby said y'all didn't have any.

MARGARET. He should know that, he's kind of an idiot.

ROXANNE. That's not nice to say! Bobby's a good boy. He's working hard.

MARGARET. I'll throw a couple packets in.

ROXANNE. Are they the little clear packets? They're clear on one side and white on the other side?

MARGARET. Yeah.

ROXANNE. I don't know why they wanna make 'em clear like that. Do you?

MARGARET. No.

ROXANNE. Makes the relish look all nasty. Like it's some kind of specimen. Nobody needs to see that.

MARGARET. …

ROXANNE. Those clear packets. Someone got paid to come up with that bullshit.

MARGARET. …

ROXANNE. I'll just go to the Wendy's and ask if they can put some pickle relish on my burger.

If I order a Frosty do you think they'll put relish on my burger for me?

MARGARET. I don't know.

ROXANNE. It's probably against the law or something, ain't it?

MARGARET. Maybe.

ROXANNE. They just coming up with laws all the time.

MARGARET. Dude, Bobby what's taking you so long with the burgs?!

BOBBY. Sorry I was just putting relish on!

ROXANNE. Bobby, you found the pickle relish?!

BOBBY. Hey Roxanne, I went ahead and used the packets and put them on the burgs for you!

ROXANNE. Don't tell me nothing about those packets, Bobby!

MARGARET. *(Handing* **ROXANNE** *her food.)* Alright, sorry for the delay, Roxanne, here you go.

ROXANNE. ...

...

Margaret.

MARGARET. Yeah?

ROXANNE. I ain't pay you yet.

MARGARET. Oh! God! I'm sorry.

ROXANNE. *(Handing her a bill.)* I should have just drove off, huh?

MARGARET. *(Taking the bill and giving her change.)* So sorry about that.

$6.44 is your change.

ROXANNE. You know what helps me remember things?

MARGARET. …

ROXANNE. Songs.

MARGARET. …

ROXANNE. If you got a song for a thing, you never forget it. 'Cause songs speak to whole other levels.

MARGARET. …

ROXANNE. Like how you know your ABCs. Don't nobody forget their ABCs. 'Cause everybody knows the song.

MARGARET. …

ROXANNE. So you need a song so you don't forget the money exchange.

MARGARET. I never forget. It was a fluke.

ROXANNE. So what? It don't take but one fluke and then you're fired. You don't get second chances in life.

MARGARET. …

ROXANNE. Don't worry I got a song for you. Hold up.

*(**ROXANNE** begins digging in her car.)*

Where that CD go?

Hey, this right here? This the joint. This ain't never gonna get old.

You can play this in a hundred years I'll come out my grave dancing. Listen close, listen up.

*(**ROXANNE** puts a CD into her CD player. A song begins to play.*)*

---

*(**MARGARET** begins dancing.)*

*(**MARGARET** and **ROXANNE** do a kind of lip-synch duet to the song.)*

MARGARET. Thanks, Roxanne. I needed that.

ROXANNE. You ain't never gonna forget again!

MARGARET. Never!

ROXANNE. Here.

*(**ROXANNE** hands **MARGARET** the CD.)*

MARGARET. Oh, I don't have a CD player.

ROXANNE. You don't have no CD player?

MARGARET. Not anymore, no.

ROXANNE. …

MARGARET. But I can listen to that song anytime I want. I can stream it.

ROXANNE. Right but what if the stream stops running?

MARGARET. …

ROXANNE. Here, take this.

*(**ROXANNE** hands her a portable CD player.)*

MARGARET. Oh, no, you need that.

ROXANNE. Not as much as you do.

MARGARET. I'm finc, really.

ROXANNE. I got another one at the house somewhere. Take it.

MARGARET. …

*(**MARGARET** takes the CD player and CD.)*

Thanks.

ROXANNE. See you next time.

MARGARET. Have a good night.

ROXANNE. Bobby, thank you for the relish!

BOBBY. Anytime!

> (**ROXANNE** *pulls away. After she disappears from view we hear her yell.*)

ROXANNE. *(Offstage.)* MARGARET, I'M YOUR MOTHER!!!!

> (**ROXANNE***'s car continues to pull away.*)

MARGARET. ...

    ...

    ...

BOBBY. Did she just say she was your mother?

MARGARET. ...

    ...

BOBBY. Gotta love Roxanne. She's pretty special.

MARGARET. ...

I have to go to the bathroom.

> (**MARGARET** *exits.*)

Three

Meanwhile. Val's bedroom.

(**VAL** *is illuminated by the light of her cellphone. She stares at it, wide-eyed. She is mostly naked. A mostly naked man is asleep next to her. His name is* **DEX**.)

VAL. Dex.

…

Dex.

…

DEX!

(**DEX** *wakes up.*)

DEX. What?

VAL. Will you hold me?

DEX. Why?

VAL. Because I'm scared.

DEX. Why are you scared?

VAL. My best friend Margaret sent me a disturbing picture.

DEX. May I see the picture?

(**VAL** *gives* **DEX** *the phone.*)

What's disturbing about this?

VAL. Everything.

DEX. Do you know this guy?

VAL. Yes and no.

VAL. Yes, because I recognize him and I've seen him basically naked. No because I don't know who he is, although now at least I know that he works at The Burg with Margaret.

DEX. I don't understand.

VAL. And when I saw him it was very sudden and there was screaming and I was in the middle of doing yoga so I was in a very emotionally open place, and that made it ten times worse.

Dex, it was so scary.

DEX. …

VAL. Just hold me, please.

DEX. That's not a fair request, Val.

VAL. It's what I need.

DEX. You can't just suddenly need something.

VAL. Yes I can.

DEX. Well, a brand new need isn't something I'm prepared to deal with at

(Checks the time.)

Two a.m. on a weeknight.

VAL. It's like you're not even a human being sometimes, Dex.

DEX. I have very specific intimacy issues, which you are fully aware of.

VAL. I know.

DEX. I'm sorry that happened to you.

VAL. All I need to know is,

Like if this wasn't just a picture on my phone; if it was him, say, coming through my window and screaming,

VAL. Could you handle him?

DEX. I'm sure I could handle him. You don't have to worry.

VAL. But what about tomorrow night when you're not here?

Or every other night of the week when I'm usually alone? I was thinking of calling off our Monday sex night – not because I wanted to. But I figured you were going to call it off eventually and I didn't want to be blindsided. But now I'm thinking maybe I've been looking at it all too negatively. Maybe we should expand it to other days. Maybe we should expand it indefinitely until it just becomes a whole life. What do you think about that? Why not just do that?

DEX. ...

VAL. Sorry.

We can talk about it later.

We can talk about it in the morning. If you want to.

DEX. ...

I'm curious about something.

VAL. ...

What are you curious about?

DEX. Your job.

VAL. I work at The Services Corporation.

DEX. What services does the corporation provide?

VAL. Well I could tell you that.

DEX. Yes?

VAL. But, you know.

The sniper positioned on the roof of the house next door would immediately shoot you.

So.

DEX. Well.

Now I'm more than curious.

VAL. Yeah?

DEX. Now I'm intrigued.

> (**VAL** *immediately takes this to a very sexual place.* **DEX** *is not into it, but* **VAL** *does not sense his reluctance.*)

VAL. Are you?

DEX. …

Yes.

VAL. Well. You might have to work it out of me.

DEX. …

VAL. I won't try to hold you, I promise.

DEX. I can't do that right now.

VAL. Why not?

DEX. Because we had sex less than three hours ago and I'm forty-two years old.

VAL. You might wanna / get

DEX. Get that checked out?

VAL. You might, yes.

DEX. I happen to think that nothing is wrong with me and that the male enhancement industrial complex has an agenda to pathologize sexual patterns which are in fact completely normal and natural. Bodies change as they age. You know what would be weird? It would be weird if I was as ripe and ready as an eighteen-year-old. I'm past that now, and thank God.

VAL. Ugh.

You're probably right.

DEX. You seem to be unsettled.

VAL. I'm just frustrated. I got myself all aroused.

I'm fine, it'll pass.

DEX. My apologies.

VAL. It's okay.

DEX. ...

Would you show me the picture again?

(**VAL** *shows* **DEX** *the picture on her phone.*)

I usually go to Wendy's on Tuesday nights at eleven. But tomorrow, I'll go to The Burg instead.

If he's there, I'll do something.

VAL. ...

What are you gonna do?

DEX. It depends on how he reacts.

VAL. ...

DEX. I'll have a few different scripts prepared.

VAL. He really scared me, Dex.

DEX. I know.

VAL. ...

...

Have you ever killed anyone?

DEX. "Anyone" is very broad.

VAL. ...

DEX. Are you talking only about people?

VAL. Not necessarily only people. But I mean.

Have you ever killed a person?

DEX. …

…

No.

VAL. You're so thoughtful, Dex.

…

DEX. I have to go to sleep now.

> (**DEX** *rolls over and closes his eyes.* **VAL** *smiles and exhales.)*

Four

Tuesday morning. The Services Corporation.

> (**MARGARET** *stands facing the water cooler.*)
>
> (*She downs her water and refills her cup.*)
>
> (**VAL** *enters.*)

VAL. How was work last night with your swamp creature friend?

MARGARET. It was a weird night.

VAL. My guy, Dex? He's gonna do something about it.

MARGARET. Do what?

VAL. I don't know. Just tell creep-boy to be ready. 'Cause it's going down tonight.

MARGARET. Okay, whatever.

VAL. Dex and I were like a Monday thing?

MARGARET. Okay.

VAL. But we did it this morning.

MARGARET. …

VAL. We did it on a Tuesday.

MARGARET. …

VAL. What's up with you?

MARGARET. …

VAL. Don't be all sulky judgy with me; this is gonna be the highlight of my week.

I'm trying to savor it as much as I can.

MARGARET. Actually it sounds like you're sort of hopelessly resigning yourself to banality and calling it good.

VAL. …

…

Well I guess, Margaret, this is my roundabout way of trying to get some commiseration from you because yeah, I'm a little depressed and I don't know what to do.

Like, what do I do?

I can't go to my pond anymore.

I can't quit this job.

I don't know what else I would do with my time if I did quit.

Probably just watch a lot of TV.

…

They gave me so much popcorn.

MARGARET. Please don't have a breakdown right now, I don't think I can handle it.

VAL. They got me. They got me to watch it all. They gave me the stream and the cloud and it all sounded so much like nature and they gave me on demand. But whose demand is it really? Who determines what I can demand and what I can't? Who is really in control? *What* is really in control? We have to find the people, Margaret. We have to find the people that we can trust.

> (**ANITA** *enters. She grabs a cup and fills it with water… She stands and sips.*)

ANITA. Good morning, ladies.

VAL. …

ANITA. Have you checked your email this morning, Val?

VAL. …

No.

ANITA. Bob and Sheila would like to meet with you.

VAL. …

Really?

ANITA. Yes.

VAL. Okay.

When?

ANITA. ASAP.

VAL. …

They sent you down here to find me?

ANITA. They didn't have to.

…

There's this quality I have. Called initiative.

It's where you see something that needs to be done. And you do it.

VAL. …

…

(**VAL** *exits.*)

ANITA. How are you doing, Margaret?

MARGARET. I don't know.

ANITA. They're not going to fire her or anything.

MARGARET. …

ANITA. I was just telling them that she doesn't feel like she has enough direction. And maybe they should consult with her. Figure out a plan.

MARGARET. That's good.

ANITA. I probably could have been less cryptic. I kind of get off on scaring people. It's a vice.

MARGARET. ...

OFFSTAGE VOICE. MARGARET! We've got a Margaret over here!

ANITA. ...

You gonna get that?

MARGARET. No.

ANITA. Why not?

MARGARET. They're just saying they need help with the copier. Because they don't want to have to call the maintenance guy.

ANITA. You're not gonna help?

MARGARET. It's not my job.

ANITA. Oh really? Do you need a job assessment meeting, too?

MARGARET. ...

ANITA. 'Cause if I had nothing to do. And the one thing – God you're sweaty.

MARGARET. It's the water. It makes me sweat.

OFFSTAGE VOICE. We've got a SERIOUS MARGARET OVER HERE! SOMEBODY PLEASE GET MARGARET!

MARGARET. ...

ANITA. Well if I had nothing to do.

And somebody asked me to help them.

I wouldn't hesitate. I'd do it.

MARGARET. Well, you ain't me.

OFFSTAGE VOICE. MARGARET!! MARGARET!! We've got an URGENT MARGARET!

ANITA. Maybe if you do your part.

I'll do mine.

MARGARET. What would that entail?

ANITA. I don't know.

Keeping you cool.

MARGARET. …

ANITA. Unbutton your collar.

MARGARET. …

> (**MARGARET** *unbuttons her collar.*)

> (**ANITA** *walks behind her, pulls her collar back, and drizzles water down her neck.*)

ANITA. Is that nice?

MARGARET. Yeah.

> (**ANITA** *blows cool air down* **MARGARET**'s *collar.*)

ANITA. Is that nice?

MARGARET. Yes.

> (*A* **VOICE** *comes in over the office intercom.*)

VOICE FROM INTERCOM. Attention, Services Corporation Employees:

We have a Margaret in the first floor office.

I repeat, there is presently a Margaret in the first floor office.

Anybody equipped to assist with a Margaret please proceed to the first floor office.

MARGARET. I might need your help in there in a few minutes.

(**MARGARET** *exits.*)

(**ANITA** *refills her cup at the water cooler.*)

(*She exits in the same direction as* **MARGARET.***)*

Five

The Burg. Tuesday night.

(**MARGARET** *is in a good mood. She is texting
and laughing.* **BOBBY** *is bored.)*

MARGARET. *(Engrossed in her phone.)* …

…

…

BOBBY. So

Just so you know,

I'm really kind of pissed.

MARGARET. Huh?

BOBBY. I said if you ever gave me that headset I didn't
want to give it back.

MARGARET. *(Disinterested, gives him the headset.)* Here.

BOBBY. Oh. Thanks.

MARGARET. …

BOBBY. Justice served.

(**MARGARET** *laughs.)*

Ha-ha, yeah. Justice served!

MARGARET. I wasn't laughing at you.

BOBBY. Oh.

Texting a friend?

MARGARET. Yup.

BOBBY. Your friend that I scared? Your real-job friend?

MARGARET. Huh? Oh, no, a different real-job friend.

*(**MARGARET** is still engrossed in her phone and remains so throughout the following.)*

BOBBY. Margaret, do you think, when you get a chance, do you think you could tell your other friend, your real-job-yoga-by-the-pond-friend, that I said I was sorry?

MARGARET. Val?

BOBBY. Yeah. I just want her to know that I didn't mean any harm.

Did she say anything today? About me?

MARGARET. Yeah, she said, like, I think she said to be ready?

BOBBY. Ready for what?

MARGARET. I don't know, she has this weird boyfriend type person, and I guess he's gonna maybe do something so be ready.

BOBBY. Is that like a…

Did she say anything else?

MARGARET. Umm, yeah.

She said, "It's going down tonight."

BOBBY. Okay, so that's like,

That's a threat.

MARGARET. I don't know. I'm gonna go.

BOBBY. What?

MARGARET. I can't tonight. I just really need to get a good night's sleep for once.

BOBBY. You can't leave me by myself.

MARGARET. You'll be fine. You wanted the headset. I'm no good at food prep anyway.

BOBBY. What if there's a line?

MARGARET. ...

BOBBY. At least stay for the eleven thirty rush.

MARGARET. There's no such thing as the eleven thirty rush, Bobby.

BOBBY. There isn't?

MARGARET. No.

We made that up to keep ourselves from getting bored.

BOBBY. Oh man.

I started to really believe in it.

MARGARET. There's no eleven thirty rush. And you'll be fine.

BOBBY. Who knew you could actually lie to yourself that effectively?

...

That's scary.

MARGARET. See ya.

BOBBY. Your mom's gonna miss you!

MARGARET. ...

That's not funny.

BOBBY. ...

   (**MARGARET** *exits.* **BOBBY** *does nothing.*)

   (*A long, long silence.*)

   (**BOBBY** *pulls out his phone and makes a call.*)

(*On phone.*) Hey Margaret.

...

Sorry I know you're on your way home or whatever I just –

...

You know you're probably gonna get fired for leaving right? I mean I'm not gonna say anything but they're gonna know.

...

Okay, well, just trying to look out for you.

...

Bye.

> (**BOBBY** *tries to occupy himself with tasks but there isn't much to do.*)
>
> (*A car pulls into the drive-thru lane.*)

Hi. Welcome to The Burg. Would you like to try –

> (*The car drives off.*)

...

> (*A car pulls into the drive-thru lane.* **BOBBY** *timidly peeks his head out the window.*)
>
> (*He takes a deep breath and gets himself together.*)

Hi. Welcome to The Burg. Would you like to try one of our signature single burgs for only ninety-nine cents tonight?

> (*The car idles but the driver does not speak.*)
>
> (*The car drives off.*)

...

...

> (*A car pulls into the drive-thru lane.*)

BOBBY. …

    Welcome to The Burg.

    May I take your order, please?

        (Suddenly the car pulls up.)

        *(**DEX** appears, menacingly, in the window.)*

        *(**BOBBY** opens the window. Then steps back.)*

    May I help you?

DEX. What is your name?

BOBBY. …

    Michael.

DEX. I don't believe you.

BOBBY. Bobby.

DEX. Bobby. Tell me something. Do you like to swim?

BOBBY. Sometimes.

DEX. Please come to the window. I can't hear you very well.

        *(**BOBBY** does not go to the window.)*

BOBBY. I SAID SOMETIMES!

DEX. I'd like one large water please. No ice.

BOBBY. …

DEX. I will pay for the cup.

BOBBY. You don't have to pay for the cup, we have water cups.

DEX. I would prefer to pay for a large, soft drink cup.

BOBBY. …

DEX. Aren't you going to come here to the register and ring it up?

BOBBY. Sure, let me grab your water on the way.

>   (**BOBBY** *gets the water. He goes to the window/ register and hands the cup to* **DEX**.)

That'll be a dollar twenty-nine.

>   (**DEX** *hands* **BOBBY** *some cash.*)

DEX. Here, you can keep the change.

BOBBY. We can't keep change.

…

We don't take tips.

…

We're on surveillance.

DEX. I'm not afraid of being watched.

Are you?

BOBBY. …

No.

DEX. …

I believe you.

BOBBY. Good.

DEX. You've passed the test.

BOBBY. Awesome.

DEX. Script B-1: initiating.

BOBBY. What?

>   (**DEX** *very suddenly reaches out and grabs* **BOBBY**'s *hand.*)

(He holds on, firmly.)

DEX. Is it strange to have a man hold your hand?

BOBBY. Kind of.

DEX. And why is that?

BOBBY. ...Because I don't know you?

DEX. My name is Dex.

And your name is Bobby. Now we know each other.

Now: does this still feel strange to you?

BOBBY. Yes.

DEX. Why?

BOBBY. Because I still don't really know you.

And we're holding hands through the drive-thru window.

DEX. Forget about the drive-thru window, Bobby. Forget all these artificial barriers that you're putting in place.

BOBBY. Okay.

DEX. Did you receive enough fatherly affection as a child?

BOBBY. ...

I think so.

DEX. If you did, you wouldn't think so.

You would know so.

BOBBY. I know so.

DEX. Your father gave you hugs? Held you when you cried? Et cetera?

BOBBY. For the most part, yes.

DEX. Bobby, your answers are not very definitive.

BOBBY. You're still holding my hand.

DEX. I know. Because I'm giving you what you need.

BOBBY. I need my hand back.

DEX. You need a healthy relationship with masculinity, Bobby.

BOBBY. …

DEX. When we, as men, perform nonsensical acts of hyper aggression it is typically because we are trying to fulfill an unmet childhood need. Even though we aren't aware of it. We act out. We scream. We yell. We scare people. Sometimes, we hurt people. But there's a better way.

BOBBY. …

What way is that?

DEX. Do you really want to know?

BOBBY. I do.

DEX. We're doing it right now.

BOBBY. …We are?

DEX. Yes.

The very simple, very beautiful act of holding hands.

BOBBY. Okay.

DEX. Now: Level two.

Bobby, look into my eyes.

(**BOBBY** *looks into* **DEX**'s *eyes.*)

…

…

…

Level three.

BOBBY. …

Okay.

DEX. I love you, Bobby.

You're a beautiful, beautiful boy. And you're on your way to becoming a good and beautiful man. And I'm so proud of you.

BOBBY. …

…

Thank you.

(**DEX** *drives away.*)

(**BOBBY** *readjusts his headset.*)

(*He stands and waits for the next customer.*)

Six

Later that night. Anita's bedroom.

(**ANITA** *and* **MARGARET** *are in Anita's bed. They are mostly naked.* **ANITA** *holds* **MARGARET**.)

MARGARET. Anita?

ANITA. Hm?

MARGARET. Are you awake?

ANITA. *(Not fully awake.)* Yeah. Are you?

MARGARET. I am.

ANITA. …

MARGARET. Anita?

ANITA. Are you okay?

MARGARET. I don't think so.

ANITA. What do you need?

MARGARET. I don't know. Maybe we could just talk a little?

ANITA. Okay.

MARGARET. I don't know what we should talk about. But I think it would be nice if we talked.

ANITA. Where are you from, brown girl?

MARGARET. *(On the verge of tears.)* I don't think I know anymore.

ANITA. Where were you born?

MARGARET. I don't know.

ANITA. Really?

MARGARET. I was adopted.

ANITA. Okay.

MARGARET. And my parents are so nice they didn't want to tell me the story. But I got my uncle to tell me.

ANITA. What story?

MARGARET. I was left in a box. I was left in a box in the lobby of a bank. Right by the ATM machines.

I don't even know my real birthday.

ANITA. Oh, my goodness. Margaret.

MARGARET. I'm sorry to tell you this in the middle of the night.

ANITA. It's okay.

MARGARET. I'm sorry to tell you this and I don't even know you.

ANITA. I'm happy that you told me.

MARGARET. …

ANITA. It's an honor that you told me.

MARGARET. I don't feel like it's an honor at all.

ANITA. Hey it's not your fault. You know that right?

It's not your fault, Margaret.

MARGARET. Okay, I think I'm okay.

ANITA. It's fine not to be okay. That would also be okay.

MARGARET. I'm okay for now.

…

I'm sorry that I woke you up, Anita.

ANITA. I was only like half-asleep, it's fine.

MARGARET. You can go back to sleep.

ANITA. No, I'm awake now.

MARGARET. You sound tired.

ANITA. I'm not tired.

...

Just yawny.

MARGARET. Anita?

ANITA. ...

Mhmmm.

MARGARET. What's your ethnicity? If it's okay for me to ask?

ANITA. *(Half asleep.)* ...

fuckin' borders man.

...

I had a performance art project in college.

MARGARET. What?

ANITA. *(Waking up.)* Oh. Sorry. I'm Tamil.

MARGARET. ...

ANITA. It's like, India, Sri Lanka, we're not a country. We're a people. You know what I mean? But I was raised here. My parents were basically raised here.

Tamils, we're like,

(Falling asleep again.)

fuck the border, man.

MARGARET. You said you had a performance art project? In college?

ANITA. *(Half asleep.)* Yeah we were gonna fuck it.

...

We were gonna fuck the border.

MARGARET. Which border?

ANITA. *(Half asleep.)* Fuckin' all the borders.

   …

We were gonna try.

But we never got the funding. And we never got scared.

   …

'Cause we didn't run the jewels on time.

   …

   …

MARGARET. Are you asleep?

ANITA. No. No way I'm so awake.

MARGARET. Thank you for holding me.

ANITA. So like,

Not to be your life coach or anything?

MARGARET. No, please be my life coach.

ANITA. Okay:

What're you gonna do?

MARGARET. What do you mean?

ANITA. You're depressed and stuff. About being abandoned. So what're you gonna do about it?

MARGARET. …

I guess I haven't thought that far ahead yet.

ANITA. Why not?

MARGARET. Because I was – I mean I was at peace with it. Sort of. It was my life, you know? I thought I just had to like…live.

Live and be a person.

ANITA. So what's the problem?

MARGARET. ...

Umm, I don't know.

I had a bad weekend.

And yesterday was like, the craziest Monday ever.

And there was something like an earthquake and it rocked all my senses and it was like...

I don't know what it was like.

ANITA. You said it was like an earthquake.

MARGARET. ...

ANITA. So you do know what it was like.

MARGARET. ...

ANITA. Continue.

MARGARET. I don't, uhhh. I don't really feel comfortable continuing.

ANITA. This is life coaching. This isn't therapy. You don't actually have to feel comfortable.

MARGARET. ...

ANITA. So, this bad weekend you had. The crazy Monday.

This so-called earthquake.

What is it that's upset you so much?

MARGARET. I have to figure out who I am again. And that's...

Hard. Because who is anybody?

Why should I have to answer that question?

Of who I am? Of what I am?

I am.

I am and I have always been

MARGARET. Since I have known that I am.

...

How is that not

A sufficient explanation?

ANITA. Who says it isn't?

MARGARET. ...

ANITA. You can't get too caught up in your thoughts, Margaret.

When they offered me this position in HR I was floored.

I could've stayed floored. But instead I stood up and I said,

HR? What even is that?

They said, *It's an acronym. It stands for Human Resources. Most people know that.*

I said, *Great, what's required?*

They said, *You, Anita. You are required. Can you give yourself completely to this job?*

And I said, *Yes I can. I'll do whatever is asked of me.*

MARGARET. ...

Congrats on the job.

ANITA. Let's get up. Do you wanna shower first or shall I?

MARGARET. It's like three in the morning.

ANITA. It's three forty-seven. It's almost four.

MARGARET. What're we gonna do?

ANITA. Go in to the office. Get a head start on the day.

MARGARET. Are you joking?

ANITA. When I wake up, like wake up wake up, I don't go back to sleep. It just doesn't happen for me. So: might as well be productive.

MARGARET. I'm sorry.

ANITA. No worries, it's fine. It's an opportunity.

MARGARET. …

ANITA. I'll shower first.

MARGARET. …

ANITA. There may not actually be a solution to your problem, Margaret.

You have the life you have. It's a question of what you do with it.

You've gotta deal with reality. That's the pill nobody wants to swallow.

So most people never do. Just leaves more reality for the rest of us, right? Drink water. And put one foot in front of the other.

MARGARET. …

ANITA. You sure you don't want to shower first?

I've never not felt at least ten percent better after a shower.

MARGARET. …

ANITA. That doubles if you combine it with affirmations.

MARGARET. …

No, you go.

ANITA. There are some Red Bulls in the fridge. And there should be a five hour energy or two on the counter. Help yourself.

      (**ANITA** *exits.*)

(The sound of Anita's shower turning on.)

*(**MARGARET**, almost in a state of shock, listens as **ANITA** sings affirmations in the shower.)*

ANITA. *(Offstage. Singing.)*
OH YEAAAH. I HAVE THE BEEEEST LIFE. I'M SO HAPPY WITH MY NEW JOB. I'M SO EXCITED TO GO TO WORK AGAIN, GO TO WORK AGAIN.
HUMAAAAAN RESOURCES, YEAH! HUMANS CAN BE RESOURCES!
HUMAAAANS ARE RESOURCES.
AND I GET THE MOST OUT OF THEEEEM
I'M GOOOOOOD AT WHAT I DOOOOOOO.
AND I LOVE IT TOOOOOOOO!

Seven

Wednesday morning. The Services Corporation.

(The water cooler is alone onstage. **MARGARET** *enters.)*

(She gets a cup and fills it with water. She returns to where she was standing.)

*(***GARY*** *enters, rolling a copy machine in front of him.)*

*(***MARGARET*** *jumps back when she sees him.)*

GARY. Hey there, Margaret!

MARGARET. Oh!!

GARY. Good morning! Do I have a contagious disease I don't know about?

MARGARET. No, Gary. I just didn't sleep at all last night. Sorry.

I feel like I'm gonna throw up.

GARY. Have you ever taken Pepto Bismol?

MARGARET. Ugh.

GARY. I find that it's very effective. Although, usually, if I feel as if I'm about to be sick, after I take it, I do get sick. But then I feel better. It speeds the whole exercise up. Which I prefer.

You really do look sick. I'd definitely recommend the pepto. Unless...are you on your period?

MARGARET. No. And that's not a question you ask someone in a work setting.

GARY. ...

I do get a sense sometimes that people don't like talking to me.

MARGARET. Yeah.

GARY. Talking is actually one of my favorite parts of the job. In fact, if I could just walk around offices talking to people while they're working and get paid for it, I'd do that. But I understand if that isn't what's needed. Over the years I've sort of – well I can take a hint – and so over the years I've trained myself to mostly talk about copy machines. That way I'm still getting a human connection to meet my emotional needs, but I'm on task. Which is also important.

But it looks like it's time to reevaluate again. Maybe I'll buy a pair of headphones and listen to old songs.

...

...

You know, it's kind of sad to think.

When I think, the thought that I think about most is that all the best days of my life are behind me. I'll probably have to retire next year because of knee and spinal problems – and so that means every time I do go to pick up a machine I think: is this the last time with this machine? Is this the last time I'll service this office? All these familiar faces, all these comfortable faces, but honestly how many of them would visit me at the hospital?

MARGARET. Probably none of them.

GARY. Probably none of them. That's right. I think that would add a lot of tension to my relationship with the nurses. They would know I wasn't getting visitors. And so they'd talk to me more. And I'd talk back. But then I would be that crazy old guy who talks to the nurses and so I'd worry about how that would look if there was a watcher at the door.

...

Well that's a scary thought, isn't it? What would he be doing there?

MARGARET. ...

GARY. I'll be back with this by the end of next week.

I left a Workcenter 3315 as a temporary replacement until then.

MARGARET. Thanks.

GARY. I hate to ask this, / but—

MARGARET. Yes, we've been using the new toner cartridges and we have been ever since you told us about them two years ago.

GARY. Okay. Because the thing is I noticed the boxes. Of the old toner cartridges. Just sitting there. And one of them:

Is open.

MARGARET. Trust me, no one has used it.

GARY. 'Cause the thing is we found those to be faulty.

MARGARET. I know, Gary.

GARY. And even if – say somebody just even once slipped in one of those old cartridges, that could cause a lot of problems. It's a domino effect.

MARGARET. Everybody knows not to use them.

GARY. I wonder why you even have them there. It's a liability.

MARGARET. It's an office. There's shelf space. Things accumulate.

GARY. I could wheel them out for you. I could even try to return them to the warehouse and get your account credited.

MARGARET. The lady in charge of office supplies is obsessed with backup plans.

GARY. Incompatible toner cartridges are / hardly a backup plan –

MARGARET. It's not a battle worth fighting. Besides, everybody is scared of that printer except me. They don't even refill the paper trays anymore. That's become a Margaret now. Paper jam. Paper tray empty. Ink streaks. All those are Margarets.

GARY. You've got the gray thumb.

MARGARET. ...

GARY. You're good with the hard plastic.

It responds to your touch.

MARGARET. I guess.

GARY. People never believe me, but I always say, you know, you have to love your printer. You have to love your copier. You have to be gentle with them.

There are electromagnetic impulses involved. Thoughts matter. It's very scientific.

You seem to get that. Even if you don't believe it.

MARGARET. I don't not believe it.

GARY. Oh, I'll be out of your hair, I promise, but I almost forgot: Roxanne wanted me to ask you if you know that she's your mother.

MARGARET. ...

Roxanne?

GARY. Yes.

MARGARET. You know Roxanne?

GARY. Yes, she said she told you she was your mother but she wasn't sure if you heard her.

MARGARET. …

GARY. Because you might have been busy working.

MARGARET. …

How do you know Roxanne?

GARY. Oh, we just kind of met.

MARGARET. Where?

GARY. Nowhere.

MARGARET. …

GARY. Facebook. Is that a where?

We had a mutual friend. I sent her a message. And she replied.

And then we started meeting at Wendy's. I guess we're both a little lonely.

We have a Frosty every now and again. And you know, we chat.

…

Well. Message transmitted. Gotta run!

(**GARY** *exits.*)

(**MARGARET** *throws her cup away. The water cooler jug is empty. She takes it off and picks up a new one to replace it. She has a hard time getting it in. Eventually she gives up and lets it fall to the ground.*)

(**MARGARET** *kneels and holds her head in her hands.*)

(**VAL** *enters.*)

VAL. Sheila and Bob are trying to destroy me.

It's a whole operation.

That's two meetings. In two days.

I can't take this.

I came in *early* today. Just to meet with them. And *they* stroll in. With their iced fucking lattes. Like everything is right with the world. Like, *Excuse me. No it isn't.*

…

Margaret. What are we *doing* here?

We need to quit.

I'm quitting.

…

I quit.

…

I'm done. I couldn't possibly go on, even if I wanted to.

I'm done.

Wow, that feels good.

I am

DONE.

…

Are you done too?

…

Why are you on the ground?

…

Margaret? Did you hear what I just said?

MARGARET. Uhuh.

VAL. So are you quitting too, or no?

MARGARET. I'm so thirsty.

VAL. I know. Me too. This water cooler is bullshit. It's probably not even real water.

MARGARET. …

VAL. I need to go to back my pond.

       (**ANITA** *enters.*)

ANITA. Oh, hey Val. So, listen: You're done.

VAL. Excuse me?

ANITA. It's not going to work out for you here. Sheila and Bob are talking with the higher ups about combining the marketing team with the sales team. You're gonna be one of the first to go.

VAL. YOU DON'T TELL ME WHAT'S GOING TO WORK OUT, I TELL YOU.

ANITA. I thought I should let you know. Before you meet with them again.

VAL. TELL BOB AND SHEILA THAT I ALREADY QUIT! I QUIT BEFORE I GOT THE MESSAGE! MARGARET IS A WITNESS!

ANITA. They're not going to care.

VAL. TELL THEM ANYWAY!

ANITA. It's in your best interest that I don't.

VAL. WHY!?

ANITA. Because of the severance package.

VAL. …

Oh.

ANITA. They have to give you six months severance. Unless they can prove that they fired you for cause. Which is kind of a high bar. But if you quit…

...

Don't quit, Val.

If I tell them you quit, the only person you're hurting is yourself.

They truly,

Truly,

Will not care.

> (**VAL** *cries...and curls up in a ball on the floor.*)

Here's what I'd suggest.

I heard you say you have a pond?

VAL. ...

ANITA. Leave all your stuff here.

Just leave it. Don't go through your desk. Don't say any goodbyes. Don't do yourself the indignity of walking out of the office with all your shit in a box.

Just leave it. Leave it all.

Let it go.

And tomorrow morning. At sunrise. Invite the people you love most to your pond. And make a new beginning.

Start a new chapter.

Okay?

VAL. ...

Okay.

...

...

Okay.

...

Margaret, will you come to my new chapter party?

It's tomorrow morning. At my pond.

MARGARET. …

VAL. …

Anita, will you come tomorrow morning?

I don't have a lot of friends.

 (**ANITA** *nods.*)

Thank you.

And thanks for the good news, I guess.

…

Margaret, I'm sorry I couldn't help you with the water cooler.

I just,

I really can't right now.

I hope I see you tomorrow.

 (**VAL** *exits.*)

 (**ANITA** *picks up the jug and effortlessly places it into the water cooler.*)

 (**MARGARET** *stands.* **ANITA** *fills a cup of water.*)

 (**MARGARET** *drinks the water as* **ANITA** *fills another cup.*)

 (**ANITA** *gives* **MARGARET** *her cup and takes* **MARGARET**'s *empty cup.*)

 (**ANITA** *fills the empty cup as* **MARGARET** *drinks.*)

(**ANITA** *gives her cup to* **MARGARET**, *taking* **MARGARET**'s *empty cup.*)

(**ANITA** *fills the empty cup.* **MARGARET** *does not drink this time, but exits with her water.*)

Eight

The Burg. Wednesday night.

(**BOBBY** *and* **ROXANNE** *are inside The Burg.*
ROXANNE *works there now.*)

BOBBY. So the way it works is, I'll be on the headset.

ROXANNE. Okay.

BOBBY. And you'll be on sandwich prep.

ROXANNE. Alright.

BOBBY. I'll take care of the fries. And the ice cream. Well, the ice cream machine is down, thankfully. But I have the fries and I have the drinks. And of course the register.

ROXANNE. It sounds like I'm not doing much of anything.

BOBBY. Believe me: sandwich prep is not nothing. Sandwich prep is tough.

ROXANNE. As long as I know where everything is, should be easy. I know what goes on all the sandwiches.

BOBBY. That's true, you do order a wide variety of sandwiches.

ROXANNE. Oh, okay, I see you got everything labeled here. That's so neat and orderly!

BOBBY. Yeah I got a label maker for my birthday and I just kinda went to town!

ROXANNE. Oh, when's your birthday?

BOBBY. It was a couple weeks ago.

ROXANNE. Happy birthday, Bobby Boy! I'm gonna make you a cake tomorrow!

BOBBY. You don't have to do that.

ROXANNE. What kind you want?

BOBBY. I'm kind of into apple cake right now, actually.

ROXANNE. Oh, okay.

BOBBY. Yeah I kinda rediscovered it. My, uh…

(Suddenly emotional.)

DAD USED TO MAKE THEM SOMETIMES!

ROXANNE. You okay, Bobby baby?

BOBBY. *(Breathing through it.)* Yeah, I'm good. I'm good.

(Pounds his chest.)

WOO! YEAH!

YEAH!

I'm good.

(Claps his hands like an athlete.)

WOO!

I'm good. I'm good!

*(**ROXANNE** occupies herself with the labels.)*

ROXANNE. Okay, so tomatoes here. Okay, onions, alright.
Alright.

*(**MARGARET** enters.)*

BOBBY. Oh! Hey M-Dawg, what are you doing here?

MARGARET. What is she doing here?

BOBBY. They needed to replace you.

MARGARET. What do you mean? I still work here.

BOBBY. Actually, they fired you.

MARGARET. No they didn't. They didn't tell me.

BOBBY. Yeah, they called me at the end of the shift and asked me to help find a replacement. So.

MARGARET. ...

BOBBY. Look, if you walk out on a job, they replace you. That's kind of standard. And I recommended Roxanne. I said we have this customer, she drives a Taurus, she's up late and she'd probably be a good candidate if she's interested. Day shift manager spots her car at Wendy's during lunch. Walks across the street. Boom. Over and out. And get this, how gangster is this: he conducted the interview at the Wendy's!

He was like, Enemy territory, I don't care let's get this done!

...

Sorry about your job, but you were gonna quit anyway.

MARGARET. No I wasn't.

BOBBY. You can rest more now.

I think, you know I kind of believe in fate. A little bit. Some part of you knew it was time to go.

Like, whatever purpose this job was supposed to serve for you: It's over now. You can move on.

> (**MARGARET** *stares at* **ROXANNE**. **ROXANNE** *pretends not to notice.*)

MARGARET. ...

...

Roxanne!

ROXANNE. Oh, hi Margaret.

...

Did your father talk to you?

MARGARET. …

What?

(A car has pulled into the drive-thru lane.)

BOBBY. *(Into his headset.)* Welcome to The Burg, would you like to try one of our signature single burgs for ninety-nine cents tonight?

…

Sure that's fine take your time.

ROXANNE. I told your father to ask you something for me.

MARGARET. …

ROXANNE. Did he tell you?

MARGARET. Are you talking about Gary?

ROXANNE. Yes.

MARGARET. …

ROXANNE. Gary is your father. Did he tell you that?

MARGARET. …

Nope.

ROXANNE. …

Did he deliver a message from me?

MARGARET. …

I don't really talk to Gary.

He annoys me.

So if he did deliver a message I probably wasn't really listening.

ROXANNE. Oh.

MARGARET. Why don't you just tell me now?

ROXANNE. Well, I think you already know.

MARGARET. Do I?

ROXANNE. Did you hear what I said to you the other night?

MARGARET. …

ROXANNE. After I gave you the CD player?

MARGARET. I heard a lady yell something. I wasn't sure who it was or what she said.

ROXANNE. …

I'll write it down.

> (**ROXANNE** *finds a pen and paper and begins writing.*)

BOBBY. *(Into headset.)* Yes, what can I get for you?

…

I'm sorry our ice-cream machine isn't working.

…

That's right. No ice cream.

…

No milkshakes.

Sorry.

I can put some milk in a cup and…

Never mind.

> *(The sound of a car suddenly pulling away.)*

> (**ROXANNE** *hands the paper to* **MARGARET**.)

> (**MARGARET** *stares at* **ROXANNE**. *Without ever looking at the paper, she rips it to shreds and drops the paper on the floor.*)

ROXANNE. I know that you heard me.

   ...

Margaret.

I am your mother.

   ...

And I'm so sorry.

   ...

BOBBY. I'm gonna go take my break.

     (**BOBBY** *exits.*)

MARGARET. My uncle told me I was left in a cardboard
box. At a bank.

ROXANNE. ...

It wasn't a cardboard box. It was a *crib*. I put you in
a crib. And there was a mobile and everything. You
was happy as a clam when I left you. I don't know why
people wanna be all dramatic about everything. Talking
about a cardboard box. *Please.*

MARGARET. ...

Okay.

But. A bank.

ROXANNE. Yes. Fifth-Third.

The one on the north side.

MARGARET. Why?

ROXANNE. The lobby stays open all night. It was warm in
there. And I wanted somebody with money to find you.

MARGARET. Do you know when my birthday is?

ROXANNE. Of course I do. The first of May.

MARGARET. ...

MARGARET. Why didn't you keep me?

ROXANNE. I wanted to keep you, Margaret. I just. Couldn't.

MARGARET. …

ROXANNE. You were born at my father's house. My mother, she had passed when I was in preschool. I don't have any memories of her. Just a picture.

> (**ROXANNE** *pulls a picture out of her bag, offers it to* **MARGARET**.)

See? You got her nose.

> (**MARGARET** *takes the picture. Looks at it. Gives it back to* **ROXANNE**.)

My daddy, he was a good man but he could only help me but so much. He didn't have any love for hospitals. Hospitals, as far as he was concerned, if someone goes into a hospital, they ain't comin' out. So he fixed up a room at the house for me. Everything you could ever want. There was a bathtub. A big bed. A sofa. And when you were getting ready to come into the world, some ladies came in. I don't know who they were. I don't know where they came from. And I never saw them again. Three ladies, as black as the night, with low, low voices, and they was singing songs I had never heard before, and they was talking to each other in some sort of secret language, and I breathed when they told me to breathe and I pushed when they told me to push, and I rested when they told me to rest, and when you finally came out they caught you and they washed you up and they wrapped you up and they gave you to me. And they made sure you was nursing good. And they walked away one by one by one, smiling at me and you. But then it was just me and you. It was me and you in that back-back room for five days. And I, uh…

MARGARET. …

ROXANNE. I just couldn't do it, baby. I ain't have nobody to talk to. Gary wasn't in the picture. He had gone AWOL before I even knew about you. And I didn't have it in me to track him down. My daddy, he did help as much as he could. He would hold you at night. Rock you to sleep. But you'd wake up screaming and I'd wake up and feed you. And before I knew it, it was morning again and daddy was at work – and on that fifth night. I said, *Daddy, I can't do this on my own.*

And he said, *If you can't do it, you can't do it.*

He's the one who suggested the bank. He had a good feeling about it, he said.

I made you as comfortable as I possibly could. I kissed you on both of your fat cheeks. Made sure you were sound asleep. I knew with someone else you'd have a chance to be okay. And with me, I knew you wouldn't have no chance. Wouldn't have had no chance to be okay with me.

MARGARET. ...

Well. I'm not really okay now either, so.

ROXANNE. Trust me. My life. Gary's life. When we were young? You're doing much, much better.

MARGARET. ...

Gary's the Xerox guy at my work.

ROXANNE. Yes.

MARGARET. We've been acquaintances for almost three years.

ROXANNE. Yes, I know.

Gary and I reconnected. Last Spring. Started sending each other messages.

That's when I let him know about you. It was the third message I sent him. I told him I had had you. And that

I gave you up. And that I didn't know where you were. I said I hoped you were still close by. But I just didn't know.

He ain't reply back for a long time. A whole month went by and he ain't return the message.

And when he did,

That's when he told me:

"I think our baby's name is Margaret."

MARGARET. …

ROXANNE. That's all the message said.

I cried when I saw that message. I cried so long.

I cried 'cause you were real. I cried 'cause I missed you.

I cried 'cause you had a name, and it wasn't the name I named you.

MARGARET. …

What did you name me?

ROXANNE. …

…

…

Destiny.

MARGARET. …

　　(**MARGARET** *storms out.*)

　　(**MARGARET** *returns with the CD player that* **ROXANNE** *gave her. She places it on the counter. She smashes it to pieces.*)

　　(**BOBBY** *enters.*)

　　(**MARGARET** *exits.*)

(**ROXANNE** *begins cleaning up.*)

BOBBY. Hey, I got this, Roxanne.

ROXANNE. It's my mess I got it.

BOBBY. Let me get it.

(**BOBBY** *sweeps up the mess.*)

(**DEX** *appears in the window, with two envelopes.*)

Oh, hey.

(**DEX** *hands* **BOBBY** *the envelopes.*)

DEX. Bobby. You and your co-worker are both invited to a gathering tomorrow morning. You may bring a significant other if you choose. So long as that other is *truly* significant. No arm candy.

(**BOBBY** *and* **ROXANNE** *open their envelopes.*)

See you at sunrise.

(**DEX** *exits.*)

(**BOBBY** *and* **ROXANNE** *read their invitations.*)

Nine

Thursday at sunrise. Val's Pond.

*(***MARGARET, ANITA, VAL, GARY, ROXANNE,
BOBBY*** *and* **DEX** *all stand at the edge of* **VAL**'s
pond.)

VAL. Thank you all for being here so early in the morning.

…

Can we all maybe say our names and where we're from?

MARGARET. I'm Margaret. And I'm from,

Here.

Who made the guest list?

DEX. I facilitated the invitation process.

VAL. Dex, can you tell us where you're from?

DEX. I'm from a lot of places.

I've lived a lot of places.

I am a lot of places.

But right now, I am here.

VAL. …

GARY. Gary. Here.

ROXANNE. Roxanne, from here.

BOBBY. Bobby, here.

ANITA. I'm Anita.

I've been here longer than I've been any other place so
I guess I'm from here.

VAL. Okay, well, I'm Valerie.

VAL. And this is my pond. And the last time I was here…

(She gets a little choked up.)

Sorry, my emotions are a little allergic. To Bobby.

BOBBY. Oh, hey, I'm really sorry about that.

VAL. I just – this was my safety zone. This was my serenity. And now whenever I think of it I think of this terrifying… I'll be okay.

Thank you for apologizing. That helps a little, I guess.

BOBBY. I am so sorry about the screaming.

*(**DEX** holds **BOBBY**'s hand.)*

DEX. Bobby needs to feel your love right now, everyone.

BOBBY. No I don't.

ROXANNE. Oh, Bobby, it's alright baby, we love you.

ANITA. We love you, Bobby.

GARY. Bobby, we love you. You're a great guy. You're doing a great job with your life.

DEX. Yes, you are.

GARY. I sincerely mean that, I can feel it.

ROXANNE. Bobby, you're the best. I love going to The Burg and now I'm working there and it's all because of you. I love you, Bobby.

MARGARET. This gathering really sucks.

ROXANNE. It's true, the first time I went in there, Bobby was out refilling the soda machine and he smiled at me.

DEX. Bobby has come a really long way to get to this point, Margaret. Can you just be here for him in his moment of need? You're not the only person in the world.

MARGARET. Thank you for the reminder.

DEX. Did you know that most people who are chronically unhappy are also chronically narcissistic?

MARGARET. …

DEX. It's a law. You could have had the greatest parents in the whole world. Who told you every day that you were loved and wanted. And perhaps that would have spared you certain pathological character flaws. But that doesn't mean that today you would have been any happier. You may well still have ended up here at this pond seeking solace among friends and strangers. We all suffer in this world, Margaret. And the only freedom from that suffering is death. And in order to achieve the freedom of death while still living, you must experience a death of the self. And in order to experience a death of the self, you must die by fire. And that fire is the fire of love for other people.

We are always perfect when we are serving others.

VAL. I waited tables for ten years and that is not true.

DEX. You never told me you waited tables.

VAL. Well I did. For ten years.

DEX. I think that perhaps you are imposing a narrow and literal interpretation onto eternal, spiritual teachings. But since I have never waited tables or worked in the service industry in any capacity, it will take some time for me to merge my current philosophies with what you have just shared.

…

I am now experiencing a small crisis of faith and have nothing further to say.

VAL. …

Well, I'm entering a new chapter. And whether that's by choice or by force, who cares?

VAL. Anita, I'm sorry I gave you a lot of shit on Monday. But it's Thursday now.

And the page has turned. And I'm turning with it. And I'm looking with hope, towards whatever is on the other side. And I'm not afraid.

I am not.

Afraid.

>   (**VAL** *takes a running leap into the pond and disappears.*)

ROXANNE. I always wanted a house with a pond out back.

>   ...

>   ...

>   (**ROXANNE** *takes a running leap into the pond and disappears.*)

>   (*A silence.*)

>   (**DEX** *takes a running leap into the pond and disappears.*)

>   (*A duck quacks.*)

>   (**MARGARET, ANITA, VAL, GARY, ROXANNE, BOBBY** *and* **DEX** *look towards the duck.*)

>   (**GARY** *takes a duck caller out of his pocket. He blows into it.*)

>   (*The duck calls back.*)

ANITA. Ducks remind me of turtles. Which remind me of dinosaurs. Which remind me of meteors.

>   (**GARY** *calls the duck.*)

Meteors remind me of earthquakes.

>   (*The duck calls back.*)

Earthquakes remind me of mountains.

Mountains remind me of goats.

...

Goats don't actually remind me of anything. I just get really happy when I think of them and I don't want to think of anything else.

...

Thank you, Margaret,

For inviting me into your life.

...

I talked to my supervisor yesterday after Val was let go, and he explained to me that intimate and or exclusive relationships with fellow employees are frowned upon, especially in the HR office.

So I probably shouldn't personally cool you off while you work on the copier. Or have you over at night.

And that shook me a bit. It made me ask some questions about my job, and what it's really for and what it really means.

If humans are in fact resources, then am I, in a way, preparing humans for consumption?

Or is it supposed to be a different kind of transaction?

...

What is this machine we're building?

...

...

Is that a question I can ask?

Does anybody really know the answer?

(**ANITA** *takes a running leap into the pond and disappears.*)

(**GARY** *calls the duck again.*)

(...)

(**GARY** *calls the duck again.*)

(...)

BOBBY. It's my fault the ice cream machine is still broken. I've been standing there,

Watching it,

Expecting it to fix itself.

Telling myself that I'm not qualified to fix it. But I didn't even try.

I decided it was no big deal.

But that's not for me to say, is it?

> (**BOBBY** *takes a running leap into the pond and disappears.*)

> (*The duck quacks.*)

GARY. Margaret, I love you.

I know that may be hard for you to believe. Or to accept.

But it's true.

Even before I knew you were my daughter.

I thought you were a wonderful human being.

When Roxanne told me that our daughter might be out there, might even be walking amongst us,

My first thought was: "Margaret. I want my daughter to be like Margaret from the Services Corporation. I wish that could be true."

Imagine my happiness when I realized that it was true.

…

You inherited my gray thumb.

And my ears I think.

And, hopefully, not too much else.

I'm honored to know you.

    (**GARY** *takes a running leap into the pond and disappears.*)

    (**MARGARET** *is alone. She looks at the pond.*)

    (*…*)

    (*…*)

    (**ROXANNE** *emerges from the pond, soaking wet.*)

    (**ROXANNE** *stands beside* **MARGARET.**)

    (*A fair amount of space remains between them.*)

    (**ROXANNE** *slowly offers her hand to* **MARGARET.**)

    (**MARGARET** *looks at the hand.*)

    (*She looks.*)

    (*She looks.*)

(Almost in slow motion, she reaches out to touch it.)

(She touches the hand as if it might electrocute her.)

(It takes some time but, finally, their two hands are fully entangled.)

*(**ROXANNE** and **MARGARET** take a running leap into the pond and disappear.)*

End of Play